AF428948

San Bernardino Man Part 1

Anthony Morrison was a smart, curious, fifteen-year-old teenager.

He was very handsome with soft, brown skin. His hair was styled with dreadlocks, that were neatly styled in a ponytail that lay on the back of his shoulders.

He was tall for his age and quite well built. He had a likeable character, with a pleasant disposition.

It wasn't easy for Anthony growing up in the East Side of San Bernardino, California as he had a difficult childhood. As there were lots of street gangs, bullies, as well as lots of petty crime in the neighborhood where he lived.

As a result of this, Anthony had a lot of anger issues that had built up inside of him.

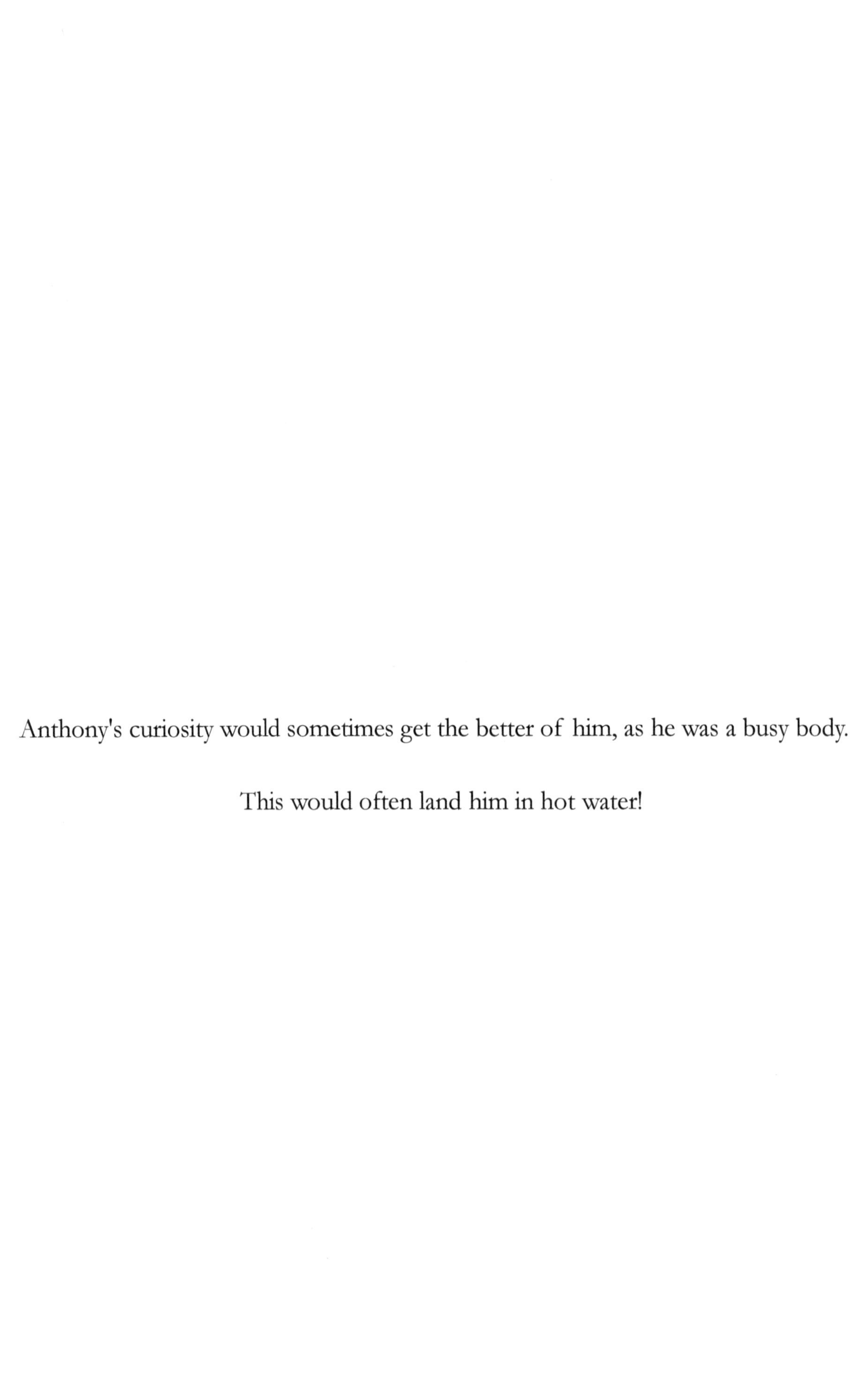

Anthony's curiosity would sometimes get the better of him, as he was a busy body.

This would often land him in hot water!

The neighbourhood children didn't like Anthony because he preferred to keep to himself.
He was a loner.

He made the other children feel uncomfortable; they thought he was weird. They began
picking on him and calling him names and started fights with him over small issues.

One day, near a local street corner, one of the neighbourhood's main bullies, Archie,
started taunting Anthony and began pushing him around.

Archie, took it too far… He blew snot into the clasps of his hands and smothered the
sticky mess into Anthony's face, laughing.

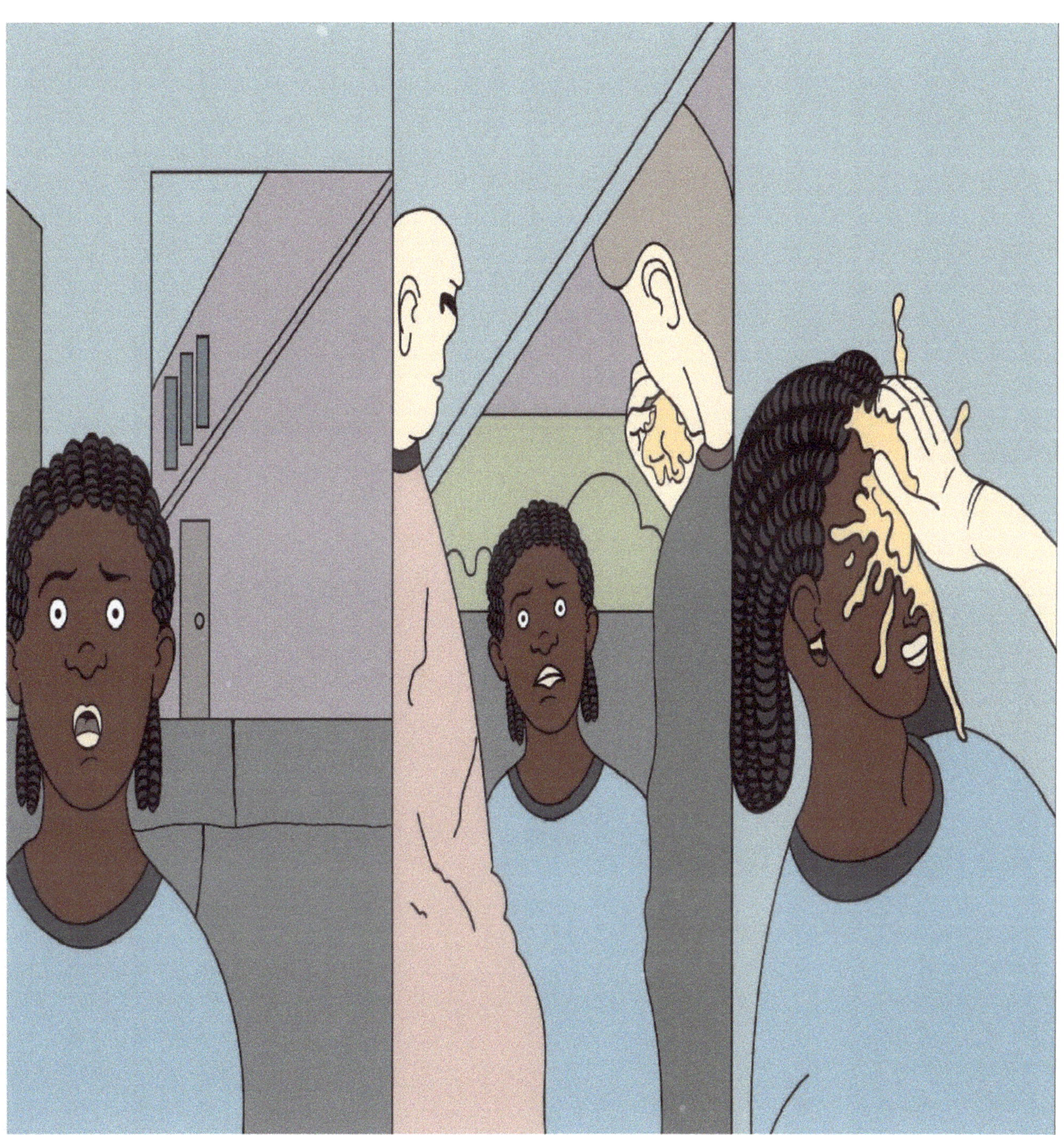

Anthony, had had enough! He grabbed a pencil from out of his back pocket, and stabbed Archie in the eye.

Anthony and Archie had a ferocious wrestling fight, Anthony gave it all he had! He tore into Archie's body with full force. He was so angry, he bit Archie on the side of his face!

As the attack was so severe, Anthony was sent to juvenile hall, a correction facility for two years. He was completely separated from his family. While he was there, he attended anger management classes. He was taught how to cope with his anger issues, as well as how to deal with challenges that he had gone through during his childhood.

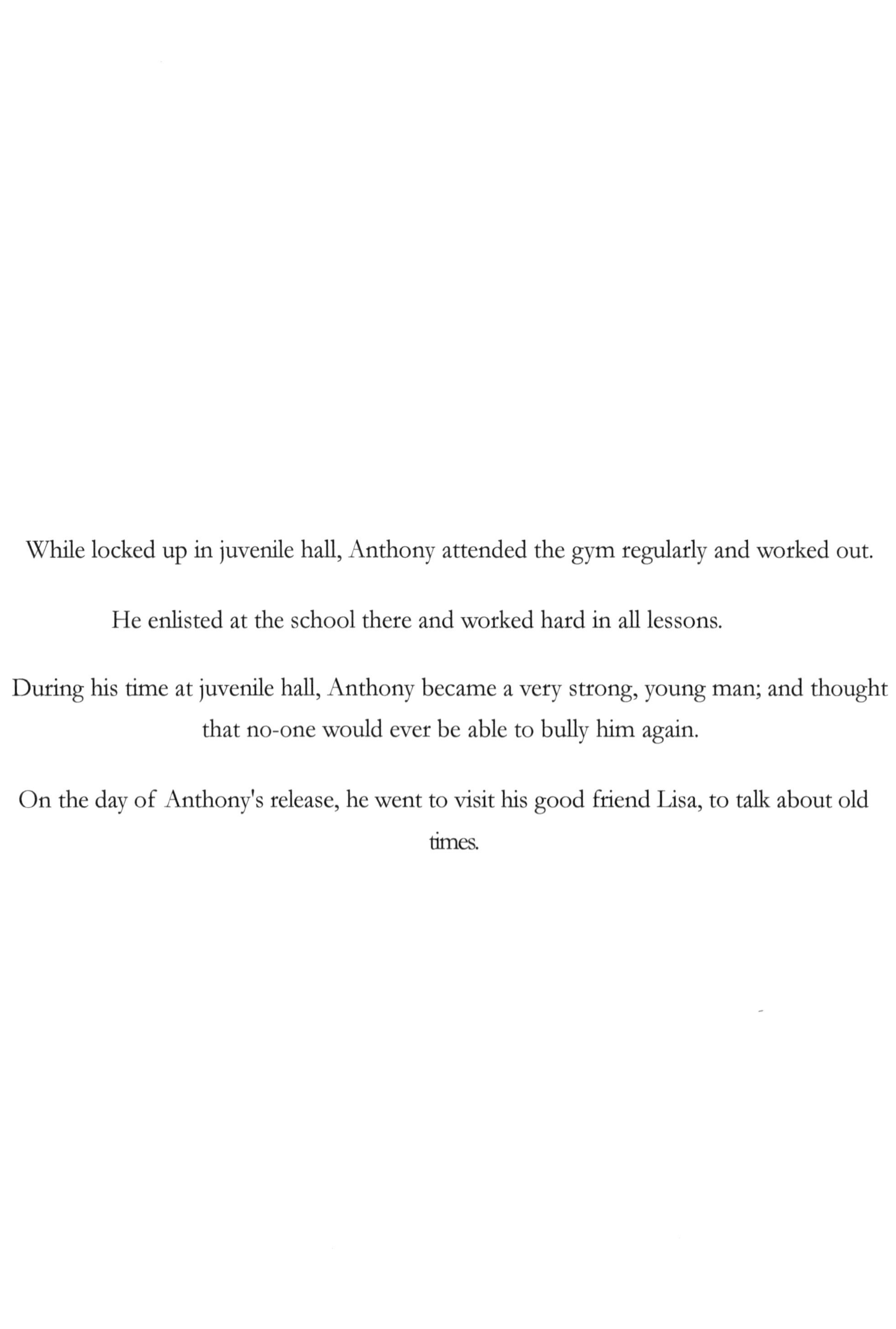

While locked up in juvenile hall, Anthony attended the gym regularly and worked out.

He enlisted at the school there and worked hard in all lessons.

During his time at juvenile hall, Anthony became a very strong, young man; and thought that no-one would ever be able to bully him again.

On the day of Anthony's release, he went to visit his good friend Lisa, to talk about old times.

I'm glad your home Anthony.
I'm glad to home, I miss you.

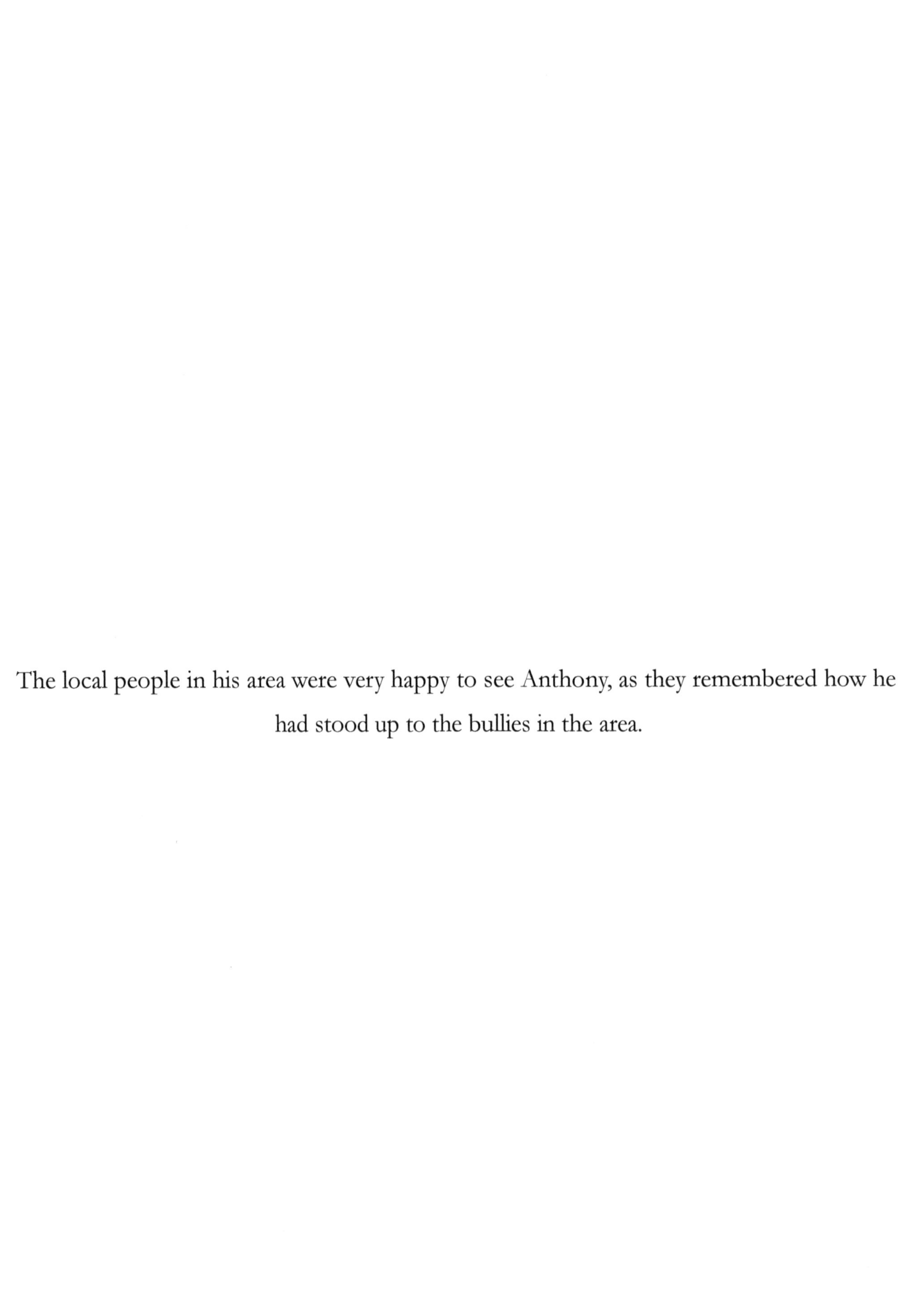

The local people in his area were very happy to see Anthony, as they remembered how he had stood up to the bullies in the area.

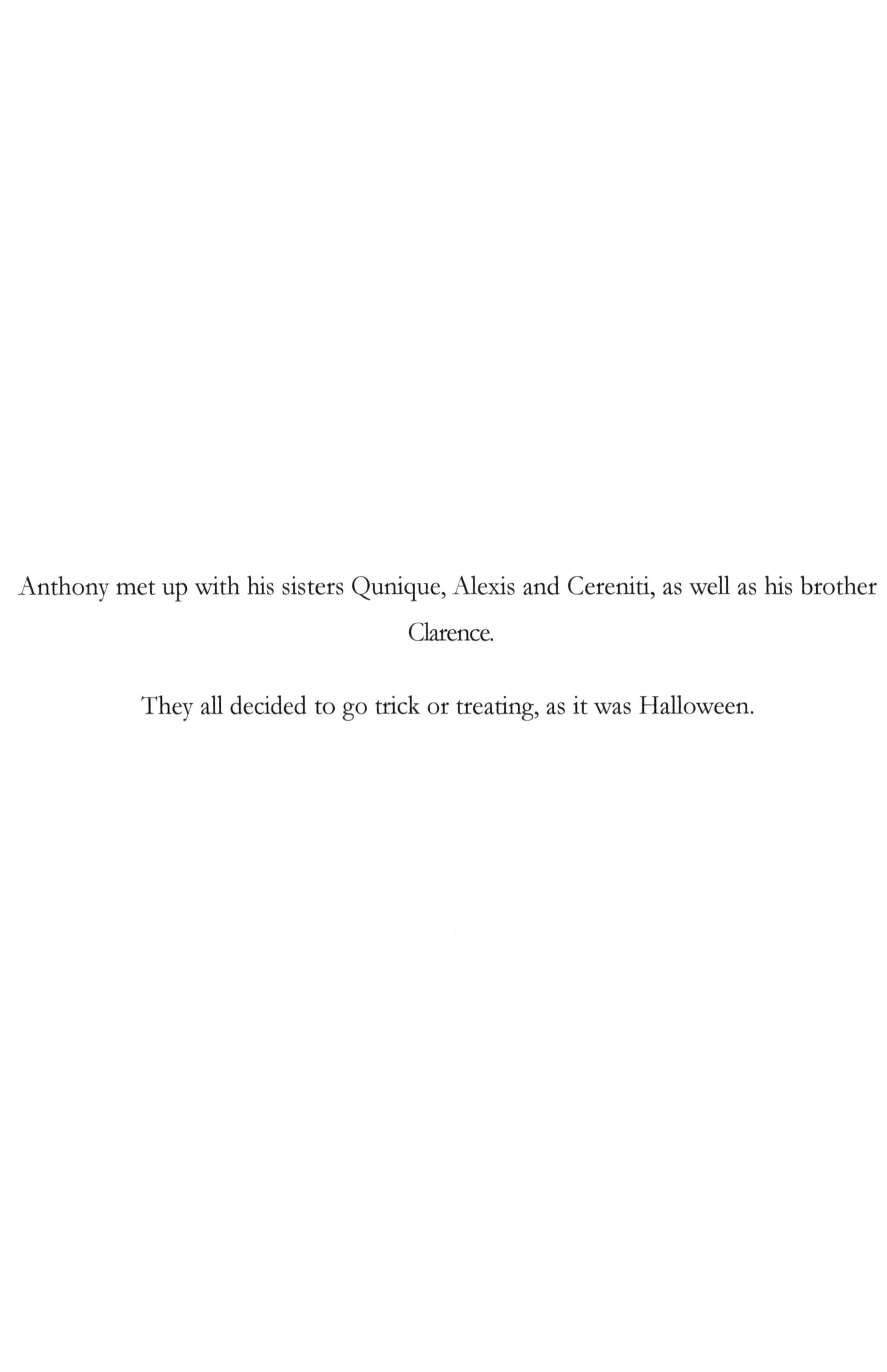

Anthony met up with his sisters Qunique, Alexis and Cereniti, as well as his brother Clarence.

They all decided to go trick or treating, as it was Halloween.

ANTHONY
QUNIQUE
ALEXIS
CERENITI
CLARENCE

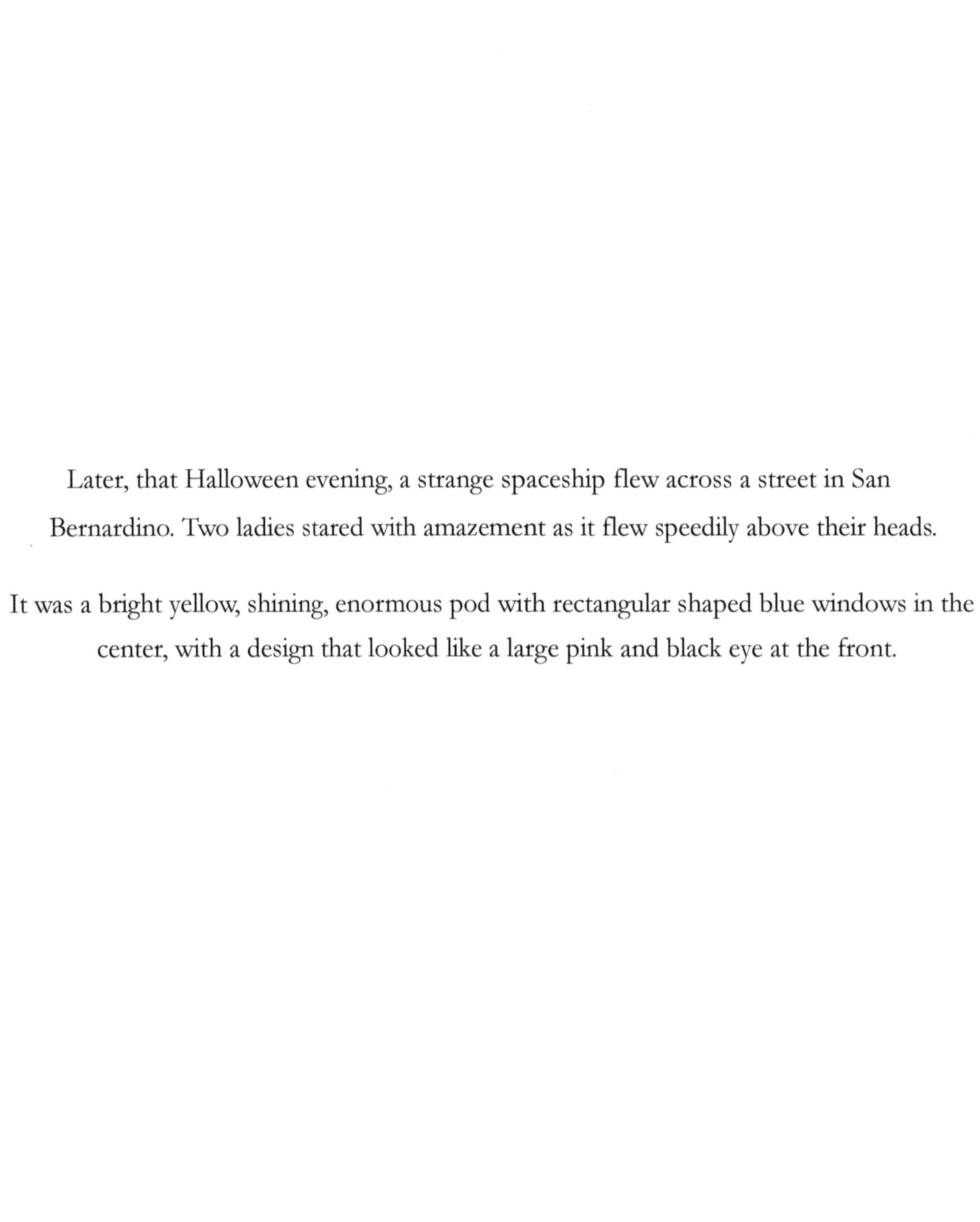

Later, that Halloween evening, a strange spaceship flew across a street in San Bernardino. Two ladies stared with amazement as it flew speedily above their heads.

It was a bright yellow, shining, enormous pod with rectangular shaped blue windows in the center, with a design that looked like a large pink and black eye at the front.

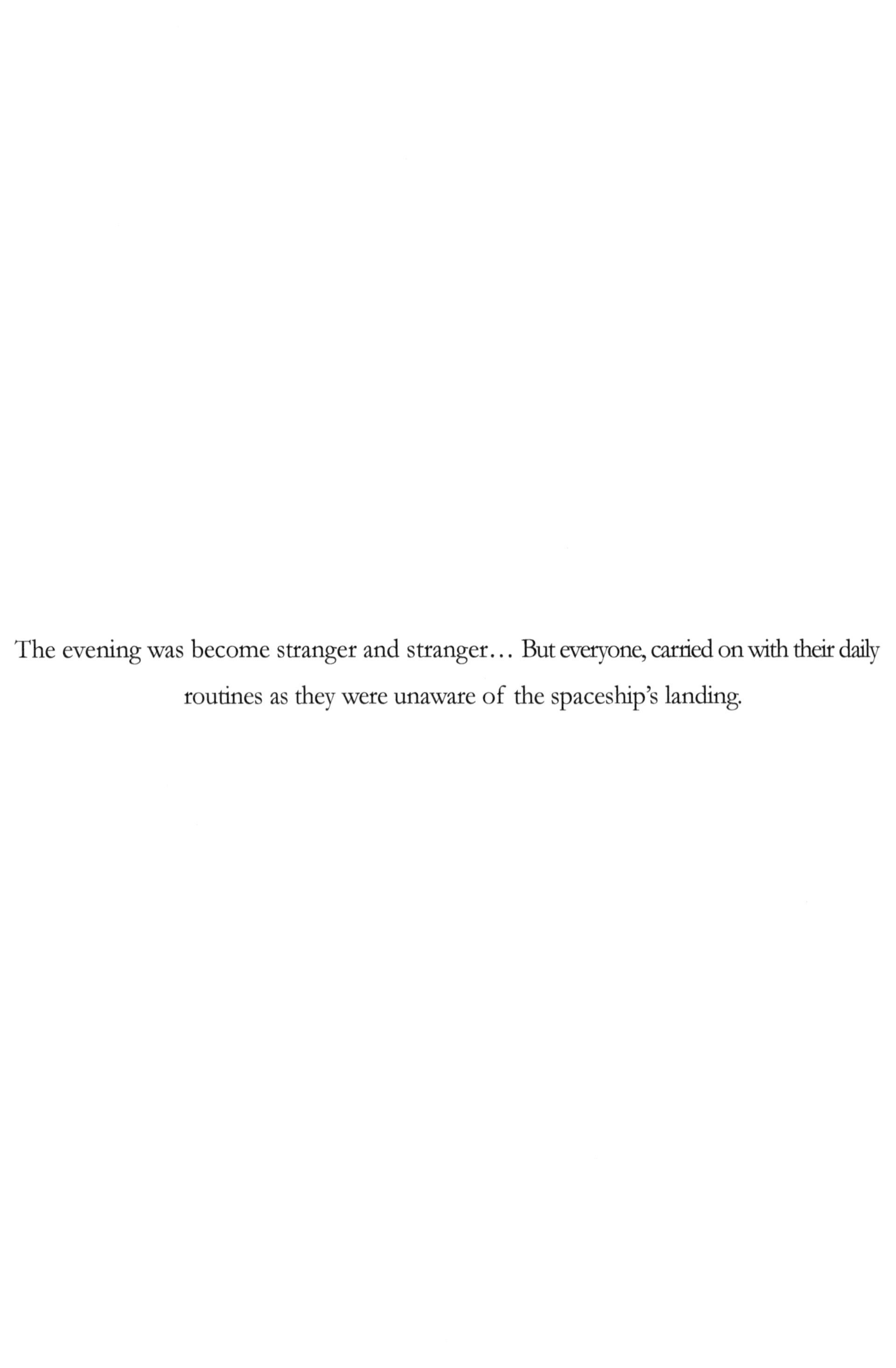

The evening was become stranger and stranger… But everyone, carried on with their daily routines as they were unaware of the spaceship's landing.

SAB LIFE RECORDS
OF SAN BERNARDINO

The spaceship landed in the Fifth Street Lake, but no-one could see it because as soon as it landed, a grey mist surrounded it, so it became imperceptible.

Anthony, his friends and family, unaware of the landing of the

spaceship, all decided to go for a ride in Clarence's blue low rider and have a good time for Halloween.

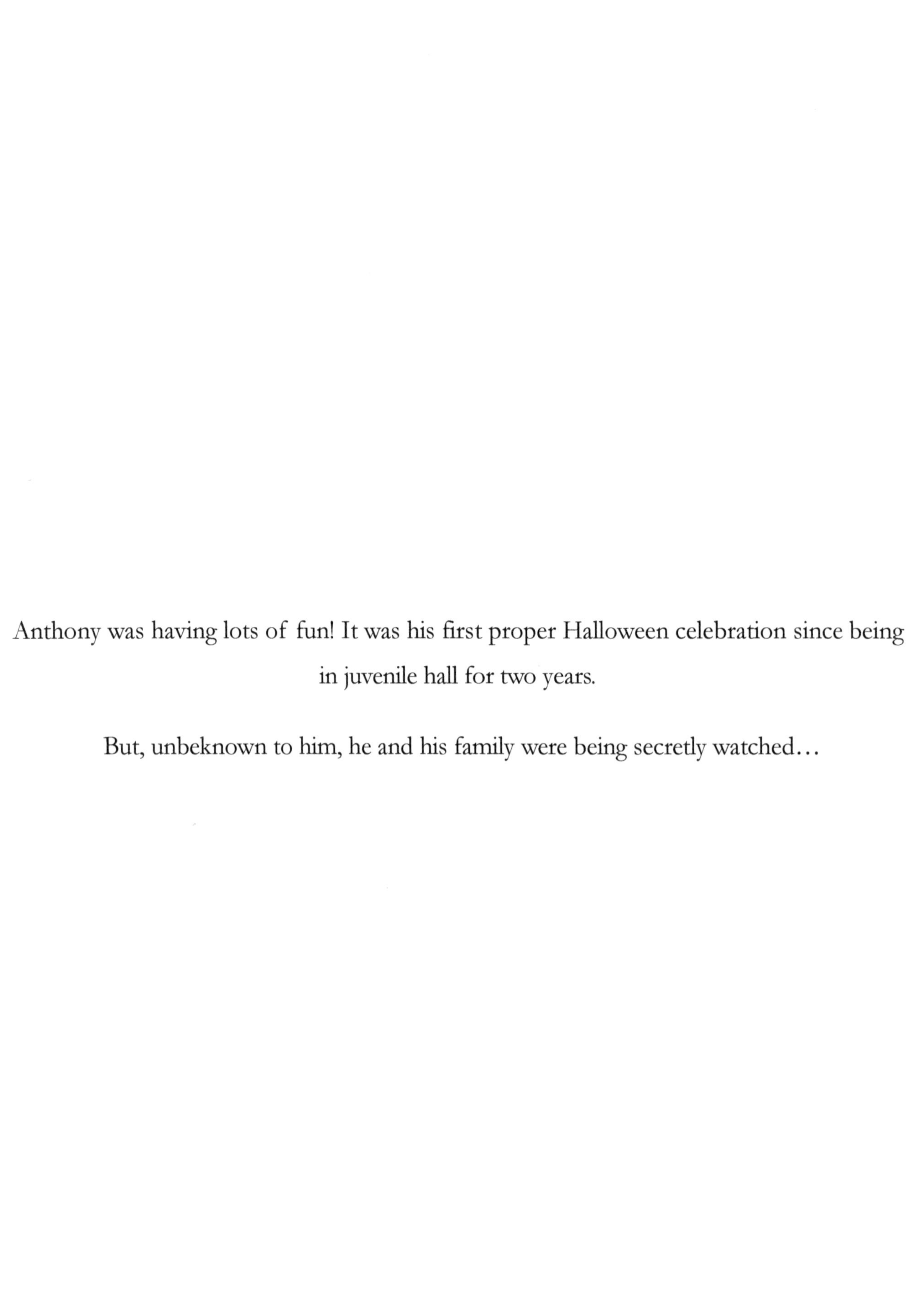

Anthony was having lots of fun! It was his first proper Halloween celebration since being in juvenile hall for two years.

But, unbeknown to him, he and his family were being secretly watched…

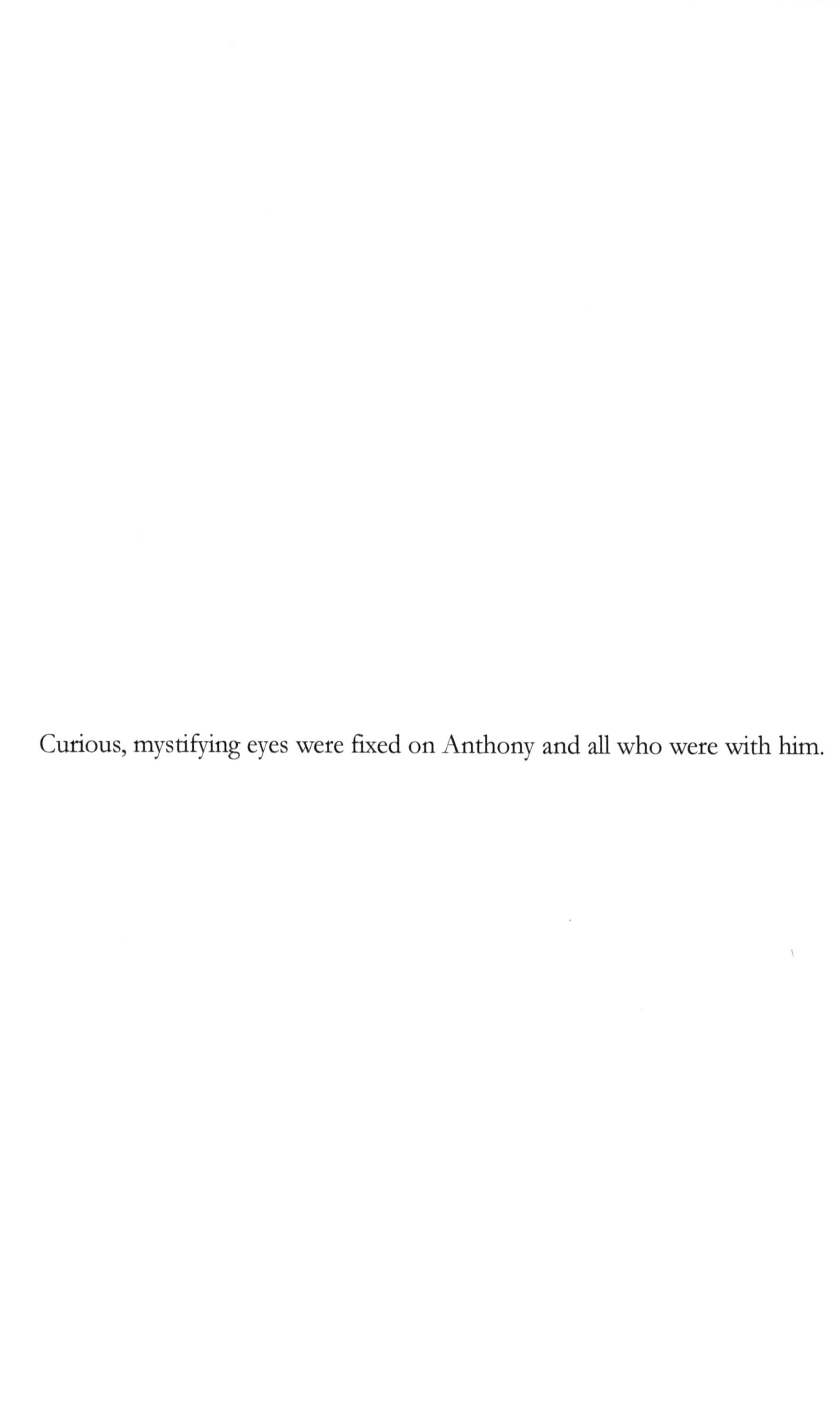

Curious, mystifying eyes were fixed on Anthony and all who were with him.

Without anyone aware of what was happening, a vicious, monstrous alien called 'Bad Nefarious' had climbed out of the spaceship.

He was exceptionally muscular, with a light, brown skinned complexion. His expression was intense and menacing.

He wore a dazzling, red bodysuit with the letters, B.N. boldly imprinted on the front of it.

He had an elongated green tail, with a spiky sphere-shaped ball at the bottom of it.

He had broad, sweeping green wings, that enabled him to fly at great speed and at great heights.

The middle part of his head was covered from top to bottom with green pointed horns. His ears were sharp and cornered. He was able to breathe out blackish-grey smoke from his broad-shaped nostrils.

He looked like a hybrid between a superhuman and a terrifying dragon.

No-one knew that this frightening creature had been communicating with Archie, the neighbourhood bully who had once attacked Anthony.

Archie, had created a highly sophisticated computer system which enabled him to speak to foreign aliens from a planet called 'FIZZ.'

The leader of the aliens was Bad Nefarious.

Bad Nefarious was looking for a secret map that Anthony's father had discovered in a glass bottle that had landed on a beach many years earlier.

Archie directed Bad Nefarious to Anthony's father's home.

When Anthony and his family returned from trick or treating, they came home to a terrible sight. Their own father had been badly beaten on his own bedroom floor.

Bad Nefarious had attacked him while trying to find the map.

HEY KIDS, IF YOU SEE SOMEONE BEING BULLIED TELL AN ADULT OR SOMEONE THAT YOU CAN TRUST. BEING BULLIED IS A TERRIBLE THING, IT CAN CAUSE STRESS, AS WELLAS DEPRESSION. SOMETIMES, IT CAN LEAD TO SUICIDE.

REMEMBER, BULLIES ARE COWARDS SO WE ALL MUST FIND A WAY TO STAND UP TO THEM.

LIFE IS ABOUT LOVE AND PEACE. STAY STRONG AND KEEP LOVE IN YOUR HEART."ONE LOVE FROM SINQUE"

COMING SOON:

SAN BERNARDINO MAN PART 2
SAN BERNARDINO MAN PART 3

Dedication

This dedication is to all young victims of violent crimes, as well as to the many women and men who have suffered from the devastating crime of domestic violence.

Remember, that there are many people and organizations that you can talk to about any violent crimes that you may have been a victim of.

I would also like to dedicate this book to the teenagers and young adults who have joined gangs due to peer pressure, or because they have been coerced or bullied into doing so.

If you would like to talk to me about any of the issues mentioned in this book, you can contact me on:

SINQUEMORRISON@Getting out.com .

I would also like to dedicate this book to my children, Anthony, Cereniti, Quenique, Clarence and Alexis; and to my stepchildren, Jayden, Jerome, Jana and Jordan.

I also dedicate this book to my grandchildren, and to my own very special lady, my precious mother, Diane.

I would also like to say a very special thank you to the most beautiful woman in my life,

Krisanne Simmons-Smith, for over four years now, we have been together. If it wasn't for your love and patience, this book would have never been published.

You have worked extremely hard to have the book published so quickly, and I appreciate everything that you have done for me.

I love you, more than I have loved anyone, you are a very smart and beautiful person, on the inside and out.

And finally, I would like to say thank you to my amazing step-son, Jayden Smith, who spent days and nights helping to publish the book.

He also helped with the graphics and design of the pictures.

Jayden, I am so grateful to you, because you helped to fund the costs of publishing the book from your own pocket. Jayden, you have a good heart and a God-given talent for computers, art, design and graphics.

Thank you so much for your help and support, I love and appreciate you.

Sinque Morrison

www.ingramcontent.com/pod-product-compliance
Lightning Source LLC
Chambersburg PA
CBHW040156110726
48005CB00018B/2780